CARDCAPTORS

Sakura's Never-Ending Day

Adapted by Kimberly Weinberger
Based on the television script by
Kathleen Giles and Meredith Woodward

SCHOLASTIC INC.

New York Toronto London Auckland Sydney
Mexico City New Delhi Hong Kong

No part of this work may be reproduced, stored in a retrieval system, or transmitted in any form or by any means, electronic, mechanical, photocopying, recording, or otherwise, without written permission of the publisher. For information regarding permission, write to Scholastic Inc., Attention: Permissions Department, 555 Broadway, New York, NY 10012.

ISBN 0-439-25187-7

™ Kodansha and © 2001 CLAMP/Kodansha/NEP21. All rights reserved. Published by Scholastic Inc. SCHOLASTIC, and associated logos are trademarks and/or registered trademarks of Scholastic Inc.

12 11 10 9 8 7 6 5 4 3 2 1   1 2 3 4 5 6/0

Printed in the U.S.A.
First Scholastic printing, February 2001

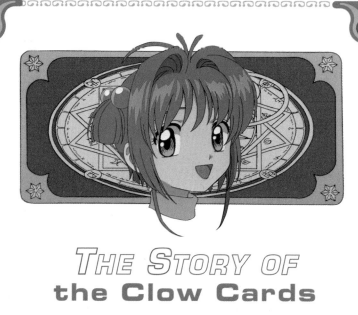

THE STORY OF
the Clow Cards

Hi, I'm Sakura Avalon. I'm ten years old. And I'm magical! I didn't even know I had magic powers until I opened a strange old book. Inside the book was a stack of cards. They are called the Clow Cards!

A man with magic powers created the cards. His name was Clow Reed. He gave each of the 52 cards a different power. But when the cards were free to use their powers, they caused lots of problems. So Clow Reed sealed them inside a book — the same book I found!

This is my friend and guide, Kero. Clow Reed told Keroberos to guard the cards, but Kero fell asleep on the job! That's how the cards escaped when I opened the book. When the cards flew away, Kero lost his magic powers. Now we are working together to get the cards back.

Kero gave me a special key to help me capture the cards. I wear it around my neck. When I say the magic words, the key changes into my Sealing Wand. I use my wand to capture the cards and return them to the book.

There's also another Cardcaptor. His name is Li Showron, a boy in my class. Li has studied magic his whole life. He doesn't think I deserve to be a Cardcaptor!

With the cards free, anything can happen. I have to capture them before their powers cause any harm. Wish me luck!

It was Parents' Day at school. Sakura Avalon listened as her father spoke in front of her class. Mr. Avalon worked in places like Egypt, digging for ancient fossils and treasures. *Dad looks so great up there,* Sakura thought proudly. *And everybody always thinks his work as an archaeologist is really cool.*

When the bell rang for lunch, Li Showron approached Mr. Avalon. Li was a Cardcaptor, just like Sakura. But he was also a relative of Clow

Reed himself — the man who created the Clow Cards. And he made no secret of his feelings about Sakura's powers. In Li's mind, she was a bad Cardcaptor.

Li and Mr. Avalon spoke for several minutes about the pyramids of Egypt. "Why don't you come by the university after school sometime?" Sakura's dad said kindly. "We have an excellent Egyptology collection."

Li could hardly believe his ears. A chance to learn about ancient secrets? He just might ask Mr. Avalon to adopt him!

Li's friend Zachary smiled. "Sakura's dad sure is a nice guy, huh, Li?" he said.

Li's excitement left him in an instant. Sakura's dad? Mr. Avalon? *Why, of all people, did it have to be* her *father?* he wondered angrily.

That night, Sakura's thoughts were far away from Li. In fact, she could hardly focus on anything as she stood outside her brother Tori's room. Inside, Tori was studying . . . with Julian.

Just thinking of her brother's friend Julian made Sakura a happy girl. She tried to look casual as she carried a large tray of snacks and some drinks to Tori's room. But as soon as her brother opened the door. . . .

"What do you want, Squirt?" Tori asked.

"Um . . . food . . ." Sakura stammered. "Eating." Her face grew hot as Julian came to the door.

"Wow!" he cried. "Pastry puffs! Thanks, Sakura."

But all Sakura could manage to say in return was, "Oven."

Back in her room, Sakura moaned sadly, "I just stood there!"

Kero tried to comfort her. As Guardian Beast of the Clow Cards, he didn't know much about boys and crushes. "It doesn't sound that bad," he offered. "Forget about it, kid!"

Sakura took Kero's advice as she got into bed. She was soon sound asleep. But a short while later, loud bells woke her. The ringing seemed to be coming from the school's clock tower in the center of town.

"What is that?" Kero asked.

"I don't know," said Sakura. "But bells don't ring for no reason."

The next morning, Sakura was late for school as usual. "I just know I'm not ready for my music test today," she said. She grabbed her recorder.

"You're going to do just fine, Sakura," said Kero. He settled down to play his favorite video game. He had gotten to the final level the night before.

Kero wished Sakura good luck as she dashed out the door. Then he turned toward the game screen.

"AHHHH!" he shouted. The screen was flashing NO DATA. Kero had forgotten to save his game!

At school, Sakura sat next to her best friend, Madison, in the music room. Besides Kero and Li, Madison was the only person who knew about Sakura and the Clow Cards.

"And next up is Sakura Avalon," said the music teacher. Sakura made her way toward the front of the room. She was nervous. Music was her favorite subject. But had she practiced enough?

"Sakura," whispered Madison. "Remember to breathe!"

 But Sakura didn't remember. She was trying so hard to play the right notes that she forgot to take a breath. Then her air ran out and she hit a wrong note. Her teacher smiled politely, but Sakura knew she had blown it.

Later, Sakura and Madison met near the soccer field. Sakura felt awful. "I wish I could go back and do it all over again," she said to Madison. "If only I had practiced a little harder."

At that moment, Li Showron appeared on the school steps. He was playing his recorder as he walked. He hit each note perfectly.

"So he can walk and play the recorder at the same time," Sakura sniffed. "Big deal."

"Sakura!" Madison said with a laugh.

Li was not exactly Sakura's favorite person. He thought she was hopeless at capturing cards. And he told her so every chance he got!

"He still doesn't think I deserve to be a Cardcaptor," Sakura added stubbornly.

"Heads up!" shouted Zachary from the soccer field. A soccer ball was racing toward Li's head.

Li noticed the ball at the last possible second and leaped into the air. He kicked out his foot and sent the ball straight into the goal!

Sakura and Madison gasped. "Great shot, Li!" called Zachary. The rest of the students on the field started clapping. Though it didn't seem possible, Sakura thought Li actually looked embarrassed.

That evening, Sakura sat with her dad and brother, Tori, in the living room. Her dad asked them how their tests had gone that day.

"Hey, Tori," Sakura said quickly. "How did it go for *you* today?"

"I got an A," Tori answered coolly. "As usual."

"Argh!" Sakura groaned. "Well, not me, okay?" Why does Tori always have to be so perfect? she wondered.

Tori crossed his long legs and smirked. "Here's a tip, Sakura," he

said. "You have to practice if you want to do better."

Sakura ignored him. Her father tried a different approach.

"You know," he said gently. "Maybe some extra practice wouldn't hurt."

After dinner, Sakura headed to her room. She decided to start practicing that very night. As Sakura began to play her recorder, Kero shouted at the aliens in his video game. "All right, Zylon!" he cried. "I did it! And I'm going to save it."

Sakura, too, shouted with happiness when she finished playing her song. "Did you hear?" she asked Kero. "No mistakes!"

Kero looked puzzled. "I thought your music test was over," he said.

"Well," said Sakura, "Tori and my dad don't think I practice enough. So I'm going to show them next time."

"Good idea!" said Kero. Then, he added, "Expect the unexpected!"

Later that night, in the center of town, something unexpected *did* take place. When the clock in the school tower struck midnight, its hands slowly moved backward. Something inside the tower waited patiently for morning to come.

"Not again!" Kero cried, staring at the screen. The words NO DATA flashed back at him. "But I *saved* the game yesterday! I did! You saw me, didn't you?"

Sakura barely heard Kero's words as she rushed to get ready for school. "I . . . ? Oh, I'm late! Bye!"

Kero howled in frustration. All that work to get to the final level of his game was lost — again!

Sakura and Madison hurried toward school together.

"So," said Madison, "are you ready to take the music test today?"

Sakura stopped short. Music test?

Inside the music room, Madison looked concerned. "How do you feel, Sakura?" she asked.

"Huh?" said Sakura, lost in thought. "Well, I practiced yesterday."

"Me, too," Madison said with a smile. "So all you have to do is breathe."

Sakura felt totally confused. *This is too weird*, she thought. Sakura turned to Madison. "But . . . we had a music test yesterday, didn't we?"

Now it was Madison who looked confused.

"Madison!" Sakura said. "We took the music test yesterday and I blew it. Don't you remember?"

"Sakura," Madison said patiently, "have you been having weird dreams again?"

Before Sakura could answer, her music teacher called her name. Once again, Sakura headed toward the front of the room.

Madison told her to remember to breathe, just like the day before. However, this time Sakura did remember. She played the song perfectly. Now if she could only figure out what was going on!

After class, Sakura stood with Madison near the soccer field.

"It all happened yesterday," Sakura said. "Those boys there . . . and next, a ball will come flying at Li. And he'll score a goal."

"Well, here he is now," said Madison. "Just like you said he'd be."

But something was different. Li wasn't playing his recorder. "Do you notice something going on?" Li asked Sakura. "We had a music test yesterday. Am I right?"

"Yeah!" said Sakura. She was glad that someone else had noticed.

"There must be a Clow Card

around," Li declared.

"What?!" Sakura gasped.

"You mean you don't sense it?" said Li. "You are hopeless. Come on, Sakura! It's in the clock tower."

Just then, a shout came from the soccer field. "Look out!" cried Zachary.

Li leaped into the air at the last second. He slammed the soccer ball straight into the goal. Again.

"Wow," said Sakura. "You're getting good at that."

"Don't you just love your battle costume?" Madison asked. She made a different outfit for each of Sakura's Clow Card adventures. And she was always there to capture every moment with her video camera. After all, Madison figured, what are best friends for?

Sakura looked down at her ruffled skirt and puffy sleeves and thought, *Well, it certainly is . . . green.* "This costume is so no one will see you flying at night," Madison said

with a proud smile.

They were standing outside the school's clock tower. Kero hovered nearby. He looked happily at Sakura. "Discovering this Clow Card is proof that you're really getting the hang of this," he said.

Sakura's heart twisted at Kero's words. *She* hadn't discovered anything. Li was the one who had known that a Clow Card was around.

Sakura said the words that changed her magic key into her Sealing Wand. "O Key of Clow, power of magic, power of light, surrender the wand, the force ignite. Release!"

She would use the wand to capture the card and return it to the Clow Book. Sakura could also use the powers of cards she had already captured by touching them to her wand. Sometimes Sakura used the Fly Card. When she touched that card with her wand, the wand grew wings. Then Sakura could race through the air.

"Okay," said Madison, "camera's ready."

"Okay!" shouted Kero. "Let's fly!"

Sakura and Kero zoomed past the clock tower. Suddenly, the hairs on the back of Sakura's neck began to tingle. Something was there, in the tower. She *could* feel it. "It's in there!" she called to Kero. "The Clow Card is inside the tower!" Sakura flew her wand straight toward the tower. But as she drew nearer, the wand began to slow down. Sakura tried to speak, but her words came slowly, too.

"Wh-a-t's hap-pen-ing?" asked Sakura.

"Time is sl-ow-ing us d-ow-n!" Kero answered, just as slowly.

The seconds ticked backward. Sakura found herself back on the ground with Kero and Madison. "What's going on, Kero?" she asked.

"A time slip!" said Kero. "It must be the Time Card. It's messing up the flow of time."

Madison didn't seem to notice that anything had happened. "Okay," she said, "the camera is ready."

"People who don't have magical powers don't even notice time slips," Kero explained.

"Does it just keep repeating the same day over and over again?" asked Sakura.

"The card only has the power to wind time back a whole day," said Kero. "And then, only once a day, at midnight."

Sakura looked at the clock. It read 11:45. "We've only got fifteen minutes!" she said. She flew toward the tower again. This time the world seemed to move twice as fast. The hands on the clock raced toward mid-

night. The Time Card was speeding everything up!

Sakura landed with a thump on the grass. She looked up to see Madison smiling at her.

"Don't tell me, let me guess," said Sakura. "So no one will see me

flying at night, right?"

"It's amazing how you just get these things," Madison said with admiration.

Kero stood grumbling nearby. "Living the same day three times is too much for me," he complained.

"No kidding!" agreed Sakura. "I'll have to keep taking the same music test!"

"You think playing Zylon Warriors isn't a test?" said Kero. "Not everyone gets to the final level, you know."

"Okay!" Sakura said. "I just know I can't stand to take that same music test one more time!"

"Pathetic," said a familiar voice. Sakura didn't even have to look up to know who it was. Li had arrived.

Li wasted no time in taking charge. "Sakura, listen," he said. "There's an escaped card up there that needs to be captured. The only way is to get another card to destroy the tower."

Madison was shocked by Li's words. "You can't do that!" she said.

Sakura agreed. "Someone in town might get hurt, Li. And people need that clock."

"Well, do you have any better ideas, Miss Cardcaptor?" Li said, annoyed. "The Clow Card's in the clock tower, right?"

Sakura nodded.

"And when you fly toward it, time goes all weird, right?" Li asked.

Sakura nodded again. But this time, something Li had said made her think. "Yeah! That's right!" she cried. And with that, she ran toward the tower. Madison and Kero quickly followed.

Once inside, Sakura slowly crept up the tower's staircase. Madison held the video camera steady as she followed.

"He's still in there," Kero whispered.

Sakura quietly moved forward. There, in the tower's main room, stood Time in its visible form. He was a stiff and bent old man, his face shadowed by a brown, hooded robe. An hourglass was held firmly in his gnarled hands.

Sakura knew that a Clow Card

in its visible form was free to use its powers. She had to return Time to the form of a card to stop him from causing problems.

Sakura took a deep breath and gathered all her courage. She raised her wand above her head and began to say the words that would turn Time back into a card. "Time!" she called in a clear voice. "Return to your power confi —"

But Sakura could say no more. Time had frozen the moment. Sakura was left holding her Sealing Wand high above her head.

"Sakura!" shouted Madison. "What's wrong?"

"I can't move!" Sakura answered.

Madison and Kero stood helpless. Then, a sudden shattering of glass made them all jump. Li had climbed the outside of the tower and crashed through a window. His entrance surprised Time. Sakura was set free. Kero flew to her side.

"Quick!" cried Li. "Use the Shield Card, Sakura! Now!"

Sakura did as Li said. She touched her wand to the center of the Shield Card. "Shield!" she chanted. "Protect me from the power of

Time! Shield!"

A clear bubble formed around Sakura and Kero.

"All right!" said Kero. "The Time Card can't reach us inside the Shield!"

Time hurried toward the tower's window, unable to use his powers against Sakura.

"Time's flying!" called Li. "I mean, fleeing!"

Sakura watched as Time flew through the window toward the tower's ledge.

Li pulled his gleaming sword from his belt. He spoke the words that released his own powerful magic. "Force!" he shouted. "Know my plight! Release the light! Lightning!"

The lightning from Li's sword lifted Time into the air. The figure

then dropped to the floor, weakened by Li's power. Sakura stared at Li in amazement.

"You backed me up!" she said.

"Now capture it!" said Kero.

Sakura held her wand high. "Time Card!" she cried. "Return to your power . . . confined!"

In a flurry of wind and light, the old man disappeared. In his place, the Time Card floated through the air. It flew past Sakura and landed neatly in Li's hand.

Sakura felt cheated. She had captured the card, not Li. "Wait a sec!" she said.

"The card doesn't always go to the one who seals it, Sakura," said Kero.

"It doesn't?" Sakura asked. "Why not?"

"Hey," Kero joked, "if I knew all the answers, do you think I'd look like this?"

Sakura looked unhappy.

"Sorry," Kero said. "The Time Card belongs to Li."

"Well," Sakura said quietly, "okay." She had to admit that Li had worked hard to capture Time.

But the smile on Li's face made her wish she could turn *him* into a card.

THE TIME

CHAPTER SEVEN
A New Day

The next morning, a tired Sakura met Madison outside the school.

"Hi, Sakura!" said Madison with a wave.

"Morning, Madison," said Sakura. "Here's hoping today's a different day."

Madison giggled. "Yeah, I guess," she said. "Although *I* wouldn't notice, would I?" Madison looked at Sakura's book bag as they headed into school. "Hey," she said, pointing at Sakura's recorder, "what did you bring that for?"

Sakura looked at the recorder and laughed. "Just in case we have another music test today," she explained.

Madison smiled at her friend. "That was yesterday," she said. "This morning we've got a spelling test, first thing."

"Huh?" said Sakura. "Oh, no!" She dashed toward class, wishing that she had the one thing she needed to pass this test — more time!